D1251961

Dedicated to Al, my childhood friend who inspired
and encouraged my love of drawing

Clarion Books is an imprint of HarperCollins Publishers.

Parker's Place
Copyright © 2023 by Russ Willms
All rights reserved. Manufactured in Italy. No part of this book
may be used or reproduced in any manner whatsoever without
written permission except in the case of brief quotations embodied
in critical articles and reviews. For information address
HarperCollins Children's Books, a division of HarperCollins Publishers,
195 Broadway, New York, NY 10007.
www.harpercollinschildrens.com

Library of Congress Cataloging-in-Publication Data
Names: Willms, Russ, author, illustrator.
Title: Parker's place / by Russ Willms.
Description: First edition. | New York : Clarion Books, [2023] | Audience: Ages
    4–8. | Audience: Grades K–1. | Summary: "A friendly T. rex tries to fit in on a
    farm where no jobs seem suitable for a dinosaur" —Provided by publisher.
Identifiers: LCCN 2022014437 | ISBN 9780358683391 (hardcover)
Subjects: CYAC: Farm life—Fiction. | Tyrannosaurus rex—Fiction. | Dinosaurs—
    Fiction. | Belonging (Social psychology)—Fiction. | LCGFT: Picture books.
Classification: LCC PZ7.1.W5737 Par 2023 | DDC [E]—dc23
LC record available at https://lccn.loc.gov/2022014437

The artist used Affinity Designer to create the digital illustrations for this book.
Typography by Phil Caminiti
23 24 25 26 27   RTLO   10 9 8 7 6 5 4 3 2 1

First Edition

PARKER'S PLACE

RUSS WILLMS

Clarion Books
An Imprint of HarperCollinsPublishers

It was just another sunny day
on the farm when Parker arrived.

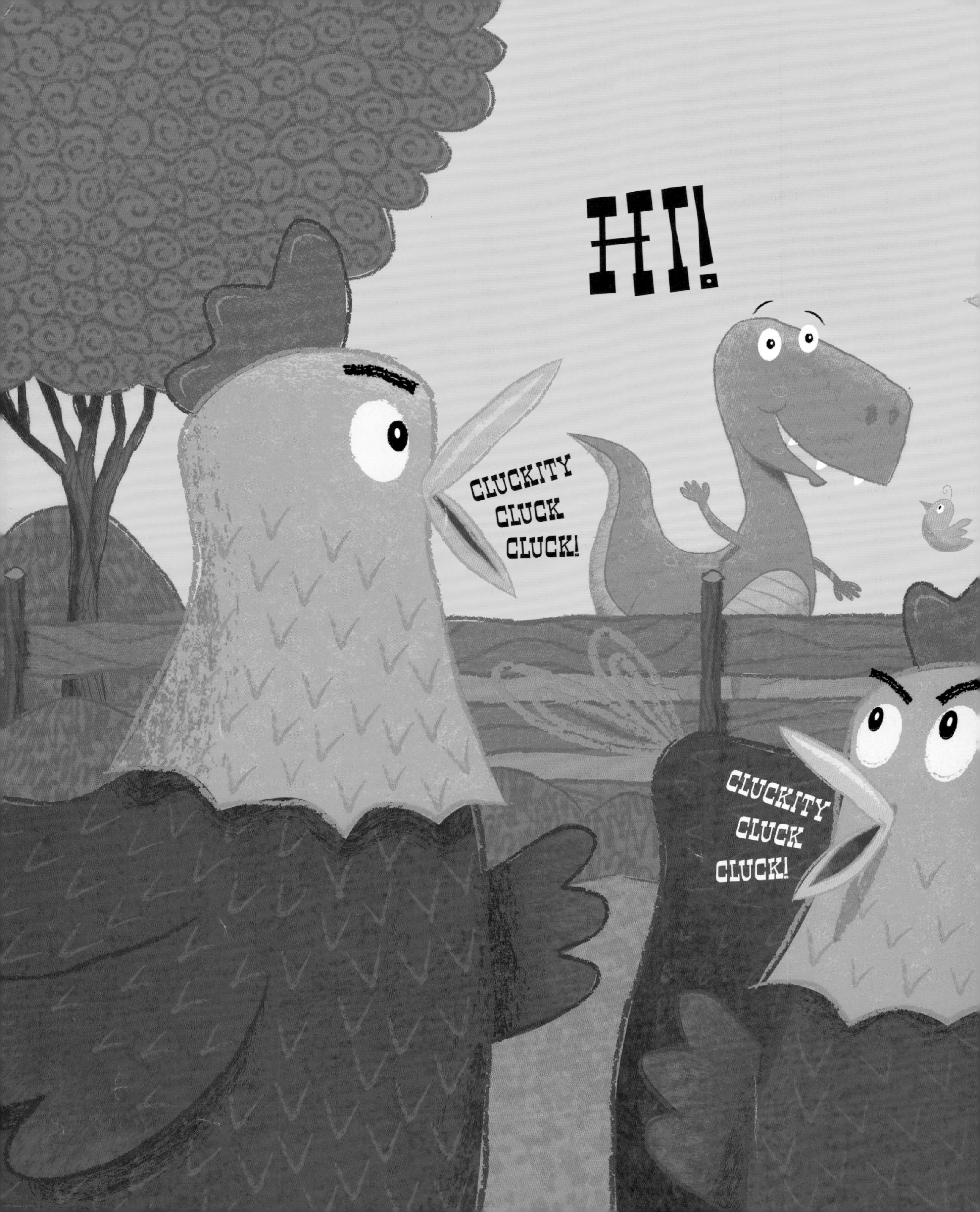
HI!
CLUCKITY
CLUCK
CLUCK!
CLUCKITY
CLUCK
CLUCK!

All the farm animals scurried over
to see what the fuss was about.

"I'm Parker," Parker told the animals.
"I've always wanted to live on a farm."

"Uhhh . . . I don't know," said Parker.
"But I'll try anything!"

So Parker went off with the farm animals
to see how he could contribute.

Could he lay an egg?

NOPE!

PUSH!

"We just need
one egg every day!"
said Chicken.

Could he pull a wagon?

Could he give milk?

NOPE!

Catch a mouse?

NOT EVEN

CLOSE!

Could he catch bugs?

NO WAY!

Could he grow wool?

NOT A CHANCE!

Maybe he could scare crows?

"I'm not sure what I'm good at," said Parker.

He needed to sit and think.

"I know," said Chicken.
"Maybe you could do some
of the farmer's chores?"

Parker agreed.
But could he give
the pigs a bath?

THAT'S A
BIG MUDDY NO!

Feed the goats?

NOT LIKE
THAT!

Could he plow the fields?

Gather the chickens' eggs?

Could he milk the cows?

DEFINITELY NOT!

Tend to the garden?

NOT WITH THOSE BIG FEET!

"Well, I guess I'll have to go," Parker said,
with his head hanging low.

"Wait!" called Chicken.
"We have an idea!"

And *that's* how Parker found his place.

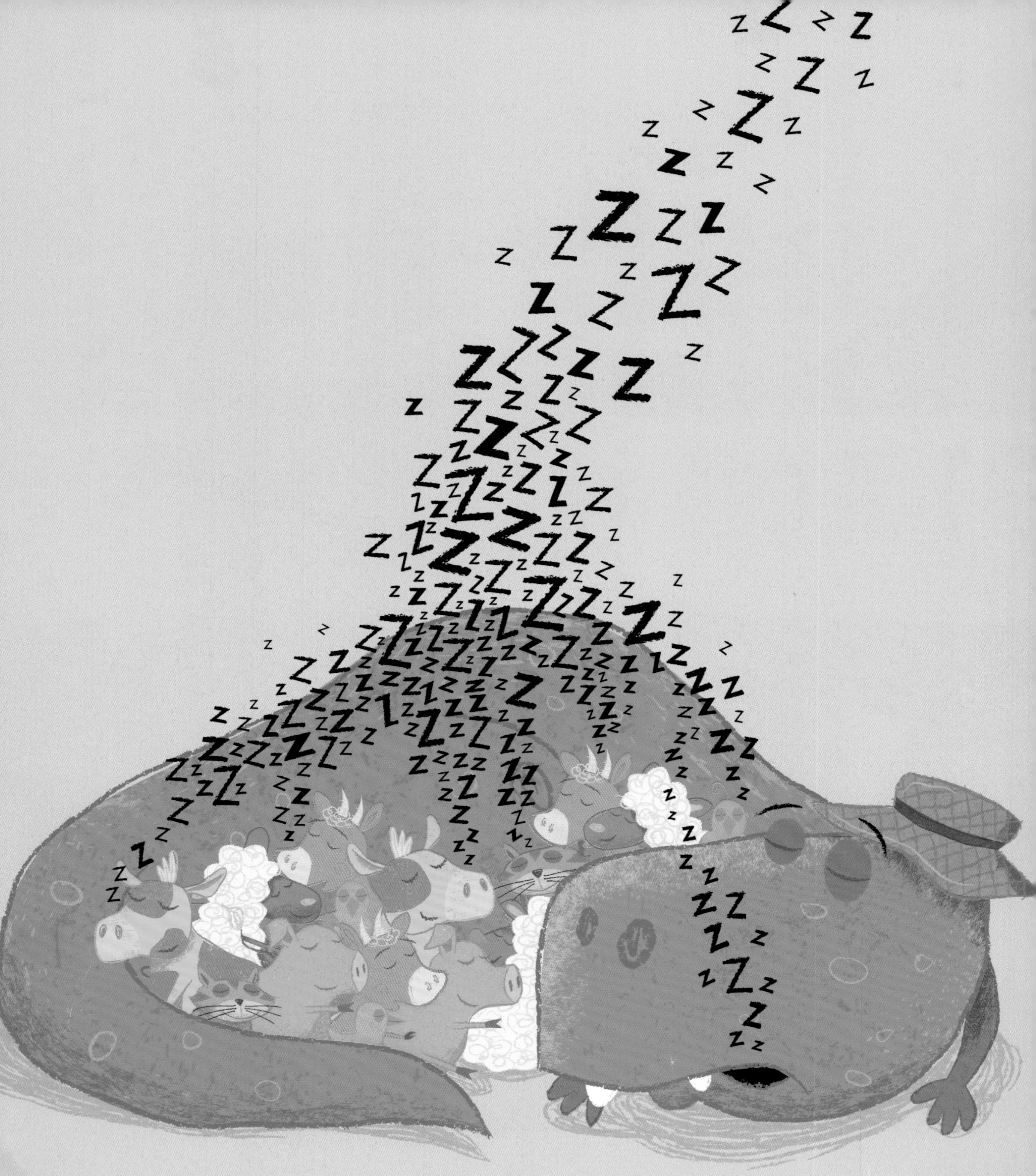